Jason and the Golden Fleece

Jason and the Golden Fleece

The Most Adventurous and Exciting Expedition of All the Ages

Sofia Zarabouka

The J. Paul Getty Museum   Los Angeles

JASON WAS RAISED BY CHIRON, one of the centaurs—those extraordinary creatures who were half man and half horse —living on the lush green slopes of Mount Pelion, in Thessaly. His father, Aison, had sent him there while Jason was still a baby to hide him from his uncle, Pelias. Pelias had played some nasty tricks to become king of Iolkos, overthrowing his brother, Aison, from the throne. Jason's parents were afraid that eventually this very bad king would turn against their son, who was the rightful successor to the throne.

Living in nature near the wise centaur Chiron, Jason learned many things and grew into a strong and handsome fellow. He was already a young man when he decided to return to the kingdom of Iolkos.

"I will assert my rightful claim to my father's throne. I cannot possibly let this injustice go unpunished," he said to Chiron one day, and off he went. Along the way he came to a river, and he sat down on the bank to rest awhile. His golden hair shone so much in the bright sunshine that it caught the eye of the goddess Hera from high above. Hera bent down to earth to see what had dazzled her so and was astonished by Jason's beauty. She transformed herself into a helpless old lady and appeared on the riverbank, pretending that she found it difficult to cross the waters.

"Don't fret, my good old lady, I'll help you cross the river by carrying you in my arms," Jason told her. He got into the river and lifted her up. When he reached the opposite bank, he noticed that he had lost one of his sandals, which had gotten stuck in the mud at the bottom of the river.

"Thank you very much, my boy," said the old lady. "May the goddess Hera protect you forever."

Jason arrived at Iolkos and made his way toward the market, which, at that time of day, was crowded with people. Everyone there noticed his good looks and the fact that he was wearing only one sandal. Bit by bit, a group of people swarmed around him. They started asking him who he was and where he came from. Shortly, he saw Pelias approaching from afar, riding his white horse. As soon as he saw Jason, Pelias pulled on the reins to bring his stallion to a halt and remained there, petrified. He was terrified not because he recognized his brother's son but because, according to an oracle, he should be "afraid of the one-sandaled man."

"Who is this young man, and what brings him to our city?" he demanded. The throng of people pulled back, and Jason, who by then had heard that the man staring at him was the king, approached and grabbed the reins of Pelias's horse.

"I am your brother's son, that's who I am. I am the one to whom the throne you sit on really belongs."

Pelias pretended that he was greatly pleased that his nephew Jason had appeared so unexpectedly.

"Indeed, my boy, the throne is yours, by all means! That is right and just," he said, loud enough to be heard by everyone in the crowd.

"However, first you should prove that you are capable of so high a post. Come, come now, let us go together to the palace. I want to ask you to do a heroic act in my place, because old and feeble as I am, I cannot do it."

Jason took the bait and became caught in Pelias's trap. He felt flattered by his uncle's words. "Nothing is impossible for me," he replied.

"I want you to bring me the Golden Fleece," said the king.
"I had a dream the other night," he continued. "In it my dead son,
Phrixos, buried in a foreign land, told me that his soul could
return home only when the Golden Fleece is in my hands. High
on an oak tree, in the distant land of Kolchis, near King Aeëtes'
palace, hangs the Golden Fleece of the ram that carried your
cousin Phrixos away to that place. And it is guarded, day and
night, by a fearful dragon who never sleeps," concluded the king.

Shrewd Pelias was more than certain that Jason would never
come back alive from this adventure. The terrible sleepless dragon
and the long, dangerous journey were not the only obstacles.
Aeëtes, the king of Kolchis, would never allow anyone to take from
him the treasure that had reached his country so unexpectedly, as
if it had dropped from the heavens.

Very many years ago, in Thessaly, two little children, Phrixos
and Helle, lost their mother, Nephele. Shortly thereafter, their
father, Athamas, ruler of the country, remarried. Ino, their
stepmother, was looking for a way to get rid of the two youngsters.
Soon the land had a disastrous year; the entire harvest was
destroyed, and people starved to death. So Ino persuaded the king
to sacrifice his children in order to appease the wrath of the gods.

It was a terrible decision for the poor father, but what else could
he do? Could he let his people starve? Or could he risk losing his
throne instead? Heavy though his heart was, he set up a sacrificial
altar and placed his two innocent, unsuspecting children on it.
But Zeus, father of all the gods, took pity on them. Suddenly,
a golden-winged ram came from the sky down to earth. The ram
landed next to the two siblings and, speaking with a human voice,
asked them to climb on his back. So, in front of everyone's astonished eyes, Phrixos and Helle flew away and were gone in a flash.

Still, it wasn't meant for both children to be spared an untimely death. While flying over the sea just above the Straits of Bosporus, young Helle tried to look behind, lost her balance, fell into the choppy waters, and drowned. Because of this mishap, the area was named after Helle and has since been known as Hellespont, or Helle's Sea.

After losing his sister, Phrixos, though awfully sad, continued his journey riding on the back of the ram with the golden fleece and arrived in Kolchis, where he was warmly welcomed by the local king. There he lived and grew up alongside the king's children, and later on he married the king's daughter. The ram with the golden fleece was sacrificed to the gods, and its fleece was kept as an amulet—a good luck charm—and as a sign of heavenly blessing for the people of the area.

Jason asked the best boat builders and local artisans to build him a strong and fast-moving ship. Secretly and behind Jason's back, King Pelias bribed the head of the boat builder's gang, ordering him to leave the fitting pegs of the ship very loose so that the already risky voyage would become even more dangerous. However, the goddess Hera, Jason's protector, sent the goddess Athena to oversee the proper building of the ship.

As soon as the fifty-oared vessel was finished, it was named the *Argo*, and Jason began looking for a crew. Although the voyage he planned was a very long and difficult one, hosts of young men of both godly and mortal origins rushed to Iolkos from all parts of Greece, all of them ready and willing to follow Jason on his daring expedition. They became the Argonauts—Jason's sailing companions. Even Herakles himself, one of Zeus's offspring, came to join the crew, as did the brothers Kalais and Zetes, the two winged sons of Boreas, the north wind. Also joining was Orpheus, son of the god Apollo and a great master of music, poetry, and singing. Jason took command of the ship, and one of the mortals, a man named Tiphys, who had been instructed in the art of sailing by the goddess Athena herself, took up the rudder and was made helmsman of the *Argo*. Eventually, he was replaced by another man, called Angaeus, because Tiphys fell gravely ill and died during the voyage.

There were two seers, named Idmon and Mopsos, aboard the *Argo*. Also serving in the crew was a man famous for his strong eyesight; he could see as far and as clearly as through a telescope. His name was Lynkeus, and his gaze could reach even below the ground and beyond the clouds. This man always sat on the bow, and as soon as he caught sight of land, he would warn the helmsman.

Among the Argonauts endowed with special traits were some uniquely gifted fellows, such as Aithalidis, the preacher, who never forgot a single thing; Periklymenos, who could transform himself

Iolkos

at will into anything he wanted; and Euphemos, who was able to walk on the waters. Rumor had it that the Argonauts were fifty altogether—as many as the oars of the *Argo*, that is—and each and every one of them possessed his own very special quality.

Finally, everything was ready for departure. After offering the customary sacrifice to the gods, the Argonauts set off one morning. They sailed out in deep and open waters, crossing the Aegean Sea. But then they hit a violent storm and were forced to seek refuge in the first harbor they came across, which happened to be the island of Lemnos. There they remained moored waiting for the weather to improve, and during that period Jason made the acquaintance of Hypsipyle, the young and pretty daughter of the king of Lemnos. Falling crazily in love with her, he did not want to leave either the girl or the island behind when the time came. Herakles got very upset by this delay and protested strongly. One way or another, Jason came back to his senses, and the *Argo* sailed once more into now calm waters, called on two more islands along the way, and, at long last, arrived at the harbor of Troy.

Great calamity had hit the city of Troy. A sea monster appeared every so often, rising from the waves. The fearful creature would make a dash onto the shore, snatch people, and eat them alive. He also would destroy all the crops of the land. The local people, terrified, remained hidden in their houses and were slowly dying of starvation. Then, one day, the king of Troy, Laomedon, sent his envoys to the Oracle of Apollo in Delphi to ask how they could get rid of the terrible monster.

"You must sacrifice your only daughter," was the oracle's reply. So the hapless king had to carry his daughter, Esione, onto the beach and tie her to a stake so that she would be the first to be encountered and swallowed up by the sea monster the next time it came out of the water.

As the terrified young girl fixed her eyes on the sea, waiting for the monster to appear, she caught sight of a ship nearing the shore! The ship sailed in and dropped anchor in front of her. Jason, the first to jump out of the vessel, ran toward her. He untied her bonds and freed her, and she in turn related to him the predicament of her city. Herakles asked his companions to escort the girl back to her father. Then Herakles himself took her place on the beach and watched for the monster. He did not have to wait long. As soon as the monster surfaced above the sea, Herakles grabbed it by the throat. Twisting its head twice around its neck, he choked the monster to death.

King Laomedon was so pleased at the outcome that he offered Herakles his most beautiful royal mares as a present.

"I will wait for you," Esione told Herakles. "As soon as you return from Kolchis, I will be ready to follow you, no matter where you may go."

The *Argo* and the Argonauts continued their voyage. They crossed the Hellespont and entered the area of Propontis, also known now as the Sea of Marmara. Then they reached the port of Kyzikos, in the country of the Doliones. The local king, also named Kyzikos, offered them hospitality and treated them very kindly and generously. He also showed them a mountain, telling them that if they managed to climb up to the top, they could have a clear view of the route for the rest of their journey. The following morning, the Argonauts, escorted by a local guide, set out to climb the mountain, leaving behind only Herakles with a few companions to look after their ship.

Come sunset, the *Argo* prepared to sail, and everyone warmly thanked King Kyzikos for all his help and hospitality. Alas, though! This good king was destined to be killed at the hands of his new friends. As soon as night fell, the Argonauts were hit by a very bad storm, and they decided to return to the harbor of Kyzikos. In the dark the townsfolk did not recognize the *Argo*; they mistook the big vessel unexpectedly entering their port for an enemy vessel. With their king in the lead, they boarded their crafts and launched an attack against it. The Argonauts were forced to defend themselves, and the outcome was a very bloody massacre. Only when dawn broke did they realize how many people were killed in vain. Worst of all, among the victims was the good king Kyzikos, who had received a fatal blow from an Argonaut's sword.

They buried the dead from both sides, and immediately after the burials they organized athletic games in honor of those who had died. But the wife of Kyzikos, the beautiful Klete, was inconsolable. She took a length of rope, went into the woods, and hanged herself. All the nymphs—the deities of fresh water, forests, mountains, plains, rocks, and caves—gathered around her dead body and grieved and mourned for her for many days to come. In fact, they cried so much that their tears formed a spring from which clear, cool water keeps running to this day.

The Argonauts arrived late one evening at the estuary of the Kios River in Propontis. The night fell, and it was balmy and beautiful. The moon sent its light down to the beach as shiny and bright as if it were daytime. So the Argonauts decided to stage a symposium—an eating and drinking feast. They laid rugs on the sand and spread upon them various foods, fruit, wines, and all sorts of other delicacies brought to them by the local people. They had no fresh water, so they sent Ylas to fetch some drinking water from a spring in the woods.

During such beautiful nights, it is known that the springs are surrounded by nymphs who come out from their hiding places. So Ylas was bewitched and captured by the nymph of the spring he visited; he was so awfully handsome that she wanted to keep him to herself. She lured him, embraced him, and finally pulled him into the deep waters with her. Herakles, wandering in the same woods in search of a log to make a new oar, heard the cries of his friend caught by the nymph. He spent all night looking for him in vain.

The following morning, the Argonauts, not noticing that a couple of their companions were missing, opened sail and set off, leaving both Herakles and Ylas behind in the land of Mysia.

After that, the *Argo* crossed the Bosporus and reached the land of Phineus, the blind seer. When Phineus was a young man, Apollo had endowed him with the ability to look into the future. But Phineus had misused his divine gift. He went overboard and revealed all the secrets of the gods, which drew Zeus's wrath. The powerful god punished Phineus by taking away his sight.

And that was not all the chastising he received. Two more penalties followed. First, Zeus condemned him to live for years and years on end as an old man; and, second, every time Phineus tried to have a bite to eat, two winged female monsters swept down from the skies and snatched his food away. These terrible females, the Harpies, left him very little to eat—only just enough to keep him alive. However, as Phineus was still able to divine the future, he did not despair, because he knew that, one day, the Argonauts would come to rescue him from his misery. So, as soon as the *Argo* dropped anchor, Phineus went straight to the harbor and asked to speak to Jason in person.

"I will tell you all that is awaiting you during your journey to Kolchis," said Phineus. "But first, I beseech you, relieve me of this torture, and make these horrible monsters disappear."

Jason called Kalais and Zetes, the two sons of Boreas, who both had wings, and asked them to give chase to the Harpies and drive them away when they appeared. Then they cooked some deliciously fragrant food and laid a very rich table for Phineus's pleasure. As soon as he seated himself and tried to eat his first mouthful, a wild fluttering of wings was heard, and, quick as a flash, the horrific females had planted their curved talons on the table.

The two sons of Boreas, hidden nearby, flung themselves against the Harpies, brandishing their swords and chasing them high up among the clouds. They caught up with them, and just as they were ready to kill them, their sister, Iris, came flying over.

"Let them be," she said, "and I promise you that they will never bother Phineus again. I will send them to live on the island of Crete, with some ogres, in a cave on Mount Diktys." And so Phineus's ordeal was ended.

Before the Argonauts departed, Phineus offered them advice on how to sail through the Symplegades—the Clashing Rocks—at the entrance to the Black Sea.

"The Symplegades are two enormous floating rocks that open and close rapidly, clashing against each other in the blink of an eye. Your ship has precious little time to sail through these two tremendous crushers—exactly the time a dove needs to fly through the crossing."

So when the *Argo* arrived at the Symplegades, Jason first made a test. He let a dove fly in between the rocks, just at the moment when the two enormous stones were open. When the rocks closed again, only a few of the bird's tail feathers had been caught. The dove had flown through. The *Argo*, Jason knew, had to sail through the rocks with exactly the same speed.

At Jason's signal, all the Argonauts—strong men ready for action, with oars lifted high in the air and with Orpheus setting the pace of the rowing—plunged their oars into the water and rowed with great speed. They managed to safely navigate the narrow passage. Only a piece of wood from the stern of their ship broke off when the powerful rocks crashed closed behind them. Finally, the two rocks opened once more, and they have remained open ever since.

The Argonauts entered the Euxinus Pontus—the Black Sea. Skirting the coast of the Pontus, they sailed past the Sangarius River estuary and reached the land of the Maryandinians. It was there that the seer Idmon died. He was fatally wounded by a charging wild boar before his companions had a chance to stop the beast with their arrows. The dead prophet was buried on the spot, and his fellow sailors marked his grave by sticking into

the earth a "phalanx," or a piece of wood, from the *Argo*. It is said that, with the passing of time, this piece of wood took roots, grew branches, and became a big, leafy olive tree. Around this tree was later built the city of Heraklea.

The *Argo* kept on sailing and reached the northernmost cape of Asia Minor, where one of the Argonauts disembarked because he did not want to continue the journey.

"I will stay here," he said. He thus became the first inhabitant of a city that was later named Senope.

The last port of call of the Argonauts before they arrived at Kolchis was the island of Ares. There they met up with the sons of Phrixos and Chalkiope: Melas, Kytessoros, Argos, and Frontes. All four of them had set out from Kolchis with Greece as their destination. Just before he died, their father had asked them to return to Greece at some point in order to claim their rightful inheritance from their grandfather Athamas. The boys had boarded a ship and left Kolchis but were shipwrecked along the way and had to swim to the nearest shore, which happened to be the island of Ares.

"Come with us; let us all go back to Kolchis. There your help will be invaluable to us, and then we can all return to Greece together," suggested Jason.

King Aeëtes, who reigned in Kolchis, had issued an order dictating that any strangers arriving at the harbor of Kolchis were to be killed immediately. The reason behind this order was that some time ago Aeëtes had experienced a very strange vision. The ghost of the dead Phrixos had visited him in his dream and told him that his life and his reign were to last for as long as the Golden Fleece remained in his possession. The king had nothing to fear from the local people, but any stranger should be suspected as potentially dangerous.

The *Argo* sailed into the harbor and dropped anchor. Only the sons of Phrixos went ashore. They headed straight for the palace to persuade their grandfather, King Aeëtes, to receive the Argonauts and to grant an audience to Jason.

Aeëtes agreed to meet Jason. While Jason explained to the king how he had made the decision to organize this expedition and why he had come to take away the Golden Fleece, the king kept thinking of his own dream and contemplating how to kill this young man who now stood before him.

"I will give you whatever you ask of me, but you must do me some favors in return. You must first catch these two bulls that Hephaistos has offered me, and then you must yoke them to a plow and plow this field dedicated to Ares with them. You will sow the furrows with dragon's teeth, which will sprout a crop of giants. Then, I want you to kill all those giants, one by one, and bundle them up like bales of hay," demanded the king.

Jason rose immediately to the challenge. He had confidence in himself and knew that in order to achieve and obtain one's goal, it is always good to have something to offer in exchange.

Physical strength and goodness of heart were not the only virtues of Jason's that charmed and attracted people around him; he was very handsome, as well. Medea, King Aeëtes' daughter, briefly saw Jason as she was entering the palace. It did not take more than a single glance at him to make Medea dream of Jason all night long. The goddess Hera realized that her help and intervention were urgently required, so she persuaded the goddess Aphrodite to send her son, Eros — the god of love — to visit and strike the heart of Medea with his arrows.

The following morning, inside a temple, Medea met with Jason. She told him that if he promised to take her with him as his bride when he departed, then she in turn would be prepared to offer him all the magical help he needed to overcome the difficulties awaiting him. Jason thought, "I have nothing to lose. I will have both the Golden Fleece and the beautiful princess." So Medea gave him a little container full of a pomade made of prometheum — an herb with magic powers.

"Take this ointment and rub it all over your body, and you and your weapons will become invulnerable to any danger. You will come out unscathed from your handling of this pair of brazen-hoofed and fire-breathing bulls of my father's. If you do what I say, the giants will be swept by your sword, like freshly harvested wheat, and they will drop dead, one on top of the other, like bales of hay," said Medea.

Come dawn the next day, Jason and the twin brothers Kastor and Polydeukes, known as the Dioskouri, that is, the "twins," or the "inseparable," went to the field where the wild bulls were grazing. Instantly, a thick cloud of dust rose and covered Jason as the fire-breathing beasts charged at him. With the Dioskouri holding the yoke, Jason caught the bulls easily and yoked them to the plow. Without further ado, he began plowing the field and sowing the dragon's fangs. One after the other, giants sprang up from the earth, and before he realized it, Jason found himself surrounded by many enormous, fearsome creatures. Then he took a stone from the ground and threw it among them, exactly as Medea had advised. Agitated and confused, the giants started attacking and beating each other until they were all killed off.

Aeëtes heard of Jason's feat and immediately put into action some other plans to get rid of him once and for all. Luckily, Medea, with her magical powers, got wind of what was happening. She rushed straight down to the harbor and warned the Argonauts, telling them that they should be ready to sail as soon as she gave them word. Then, that night, she led Jason to the grove where the Golden Fleece had been kept under guard for so many years.

"Wait here," she said, leaving him hiding behind a bush. Continuing alone, she approached the oak tree with the Golden Fleece hanging from its branches. Coiled precisely at the foot of the tree, a terrifying dragon kept watch over the fleece night and day. Medea made herself invisible, bent down, and let some drops of a magic liquid trickle onto his eyes, and thus she put the dragon to sleep.

Jason emerged from his hiding place and, stepping onto the back of the unconscious dragon, snatched the shining Golden Fleece from the tree. Then he grasped Medea's hand, and they both ran as fast as they could run toward the harbor. All this had taken place in the dark, under cover of night. By the time Aeëtes found out what had happened, the *Argo* was already far out in the open sea. As the Argonauts were approaching the land of Paphlagonia, King Aeëtes ordered his son Apsyrtos to give them chase.

There were only two ways that the ship could get out of the Straits of Bosporus and start its homeward journey: either by crossing the Bosporus or sailing up the Ister River, otherwise known as the Danube. The Argonauts recalled the blind seer Phineus's advice not to return to Greece by the same route. Therefore they chose to navigate the river, and thus they proceeded in a northwesterly direction. But Apsyrtos had anticipated this move and had already sent one of his ships to lie in wait in the Bosporus, while he himself boarded another vessel and waited for them at the Ister River estuary.

But the *Argo* could not pass through. Stalling for time, Jason asked to have a talk with Medea's brother. He sent word that should they come to an agreement, he would be willing to give him back both the stolen fleece and his sister.

Jason and Medea sent a message to Apsyrtos, asking him to come alone and meet them on a deserted beach. There the pair of them waited for his arrival on the top of a precipice. Completely trusting and unsuspecting, Apsyrtos met them at the appointed place. No thought of danger crossed his mind, as his own sister was present. But Medea was the one who forced her brother to the very edge of the cliff, and when Jason got cold feet and wavered, it was she who ordered, "Kill him!" And so the deed was done.

Eridanus River

Ister River

Stoichades

Aethalia

Kirce

Sirens

Skylla and
Charybdis

Plankton
Stones

Corfu

Having lost their leader, the comrades of Apsyrtos could no longer pursue the *Argo*. The Argonauts reached the shores of the land of Illyria without further mishap.

They were already approaching Corfu when some sudden gusts of a strong northern wind sent them flying back out into the open sea. Desperately, the Argonauts watched their ship moving farther and farther away from their homeland. Then the *Argo* began speaking with a human voice. The voice came out of its prow, where Athena had inserted a piece of wood from the speaking oak of the temple of Dodona while the ship was being built.

"Zeus is very angry about Apsyrtos's murder," said the peculiar and outlandish voice. "This horrendous act of fratricide is a treacherous and unforgivable crime. You must now go straight to the isle of the famous witch Kirke in order to seek her forgiveness and to expiate and purify yourselves. After that, you may have a chance of returning home safely."

The strong winds pushed the *Argo* all the way up to the northernmost waters of the Adriatic Sea and into the estuary of the Eridanus River. Leaving behind the open sea, the *Argo* sailed up the Eridanus River first, and later down the Rodanus River, finally reaching the Sardinian and the Tyrrhenian seas. Once again in open waters, the Argonauts dropped anchor at the Stoichades Islands. Then they sailed south to the next port of call, the island of Aethalia. That island's port has ever since been called Argon — that is, the port of Argo — in the same way that a port on the Etruscan coast was named Telamonium, after the Argonaut Telamon.

Kirke, being the witch that she was, knew beforehand that the Argonauts were due to arrive at her homeland. She knew of the horrible crime committed by Medea and Jason; in her dreams she had seen their vessel sailing into a sea of blood. She agreed to purify all the others aboard the *Argo*, but not the pair of murderers. With the purification ritual over, the *Argo* now had to sail past the island of Anthemousa, which was full of flowers.

"Do not make the terrible mistake of stopping there," Kirke warned. "It looks like a paradise, but it is the island where the dreadful Sirens live. They sing so sweetly that whoever hears their song becomes completely bewitched. A sailor thinks that there is nothing in this life more beautiful than their singing and forgets his purpose and his destination. He remains there forever, with no aim in his life, expecting nothing, doing nothing, slowly dying."

When the *Argo* reached the shores of the island, Orpheus sat down in the middle of the deck, took his lyre in his hands, and began strumming a beautiful tune. Overwhelming the sound of singing coming from the Sirens' island, his music protected everyone on board from its enchanting lure. In this way one more danger was overcome. However, the perils of the return journey were not over yet. Home was still quite a long way away. The Argonauts had to sail between Skylla and Charybdis—the two fearful creatures who, perched on two high rocks, threatened and usually took the lives of people sailing by. With the help of Hera, the Argonauts managed to escape their clutches, and their lives were spared. But before they had time to catch their breath and draw a sigh of relief, they saw some enormous sea rocks floating wildly in the waters straight ahead, like boats adrift. Back and forth, left and right, the waves hit the floating rocks from all directions, and the angry foam spraying around them looked like the smoke plumes from a tremendous fire. Those floating rocks, called "Plankton Stones," were very dangerous for all mariners. Still, once more, the goddess Hera intervened and led the Argonauts safely through, helping them to overcome yet another obstacle.

The island of the Phaeakians, Corfu, was ruled by the hospitable King Alkinous, and it was here that the exhausted Argonauts chose to take some rest. They planned to stay there awhile, undisturbed and free of cares, until they recovered from their tribulations, got themselves fresh provisions, and felt ready to continue their journey. But suddenly, one day, the island's

peaceful harbor saw the unexpected arrival of a strange, oddly dark vessel. It looked as if it came from the east, and the Argonauts recognized it as one of the boats of Kolchis. Envoys of King Aeëtes disembarked and knocked on the door of King Alkinous's palace. They demanded that the king turn Medea over to them. She was now the one whom her own father—also father of the unfairly and treacherously killed Apsyrtos—was trying frantically to track down. The good king Alkinous promised that he would deliver Medea to them, unless she was already married, in which case this decision would rest with her husband.

That same evening, inside a cave, the king and his wife, Arete, hurriedly officiated at Jason and Medea's wedding. To express her joy at her deliverance and to show her happiness about her wedding, Medea consecrated various sacrificial altars to the nymphs as well as to the Fates.

Medea now left the island of the Phaeakians, together with her husband, the crew of Argonauts, and a dozen women, who were presented to her by Queen Arete to serve as her maids and ladies-in-waiting.

By the time the Argonauts were almost within sight of the Peloponnesos, another ferocious northerly storm took them off their course and pushed them south, to the North African coast. For nine whole days they kept fighting the enormous waves that ran them aground in the shallow waters of the African shore. The ship got stuck in the sands of the Libyan Syrtes, the two big bays on the Libyan and Tunisian coasts. The Argonauts felt desperate and grew even more so when they set foot on land. Ahead of them lay the Libyan desert. They fell asleep, worn out with fatigue, and Jason dreamed that three local goddesses of that land came to visit him.

"You must repay your mother, who carried you in her arms for such a long time, her rightful dues. This must be done the very moment that Amphitrite unharnesses the horses from the chariot of Poseidon, her husband," the deities told Jason in his sleep.

The following morning, Jason related his dream to his comrades, because he had not been able to make head nor tail of the goddesses' advice. The sun reigned high above them, and still no one could interpret this peculiar dream. Suddenly, the sea became agitated, and a horse with a golden mane emerged from the waters, galloped along the sandy beach, and headed off in the direction of the desert. Then Peleus — one of the Argonauts — who knew all about oceans, lakes, and seas, came up with an explanation:

"The horse," he said, "must be one of those pulling Poseidon's chariot. As for the mother the goddesses mentioned, she might well be the *Argo*, who is carrying us in her bosom."

Now it was their turn to carry the *Argo* in their arms, or, rather, on their shoulders, as the case may be. The Argonauts had to get the *Argo* unstuck from the sand, lift her up, and then follow the hoof marks of the horse, which, sooner or later, were going to lead them to a sea suitable for launching the ship so that the *Argo* could sail again.

With a superhuman effort, the Argonauts managed to get the stranded ship unstuck from the sands and lift it up with their bare arms. Carrying the *Argo* on their shoulders, they entered the desert and moved overland, following the tracks of the horse's hooves.

Utterly exhausted, the Argonauts reached an expanse of water, Lake Tritonis, where they launched the *Argo* once more. They were surrounded by empty desert for as far as the eye could see. Some of them started walking in the hope of finding some freshwater spring. Indeed, after a while, they caught sight of some treetops on the distant horizon. They approached the site and found themselves in a beautiful, tree-filled, green garden. It was the Garden of the Hesperides — the female creatures who guarded the famous Golden Apples. These beautiful young women, wishing to offer the Argonauts a shady place to rest and help them get refreshed, turned themselves into trees: the first girl into a willow, the second into a tall leafy poplar, and the third into an elm tree.

When the men returned to join their comrades, bringing water back with them, the Argonauts started sailing around the lakeshore, searching for an opening that would bring them to the Mediterranean Sea. With the help of Triton—the god of the sea—to whom Jason offered the sacrifice of a beautiful ram, the Argonauts found themselves once more in the open sea, and, with a favorable wind filling their sails, they reached the island of Crete.

No ship dared moor at this island because the oversized, brazen monster Talos, a guard of King Minos, patrolled the shores of Crete. Every time he spotted a vessel approaching the island, he sank it by throwing stones so huge that only he was able to lift them. Medea stood on the deck of the *Argo* and sent her magical gaze toward the shore. As soon as Talos appeared, and before the gigantic guard had a chance to catch sight of the ship and try to drive it away, Medea's gaze struck him. The giant dropped like a felled tree and died on the spot. The Argonauts then had a chance to go ashore and replenish their stock of drinking water. Then they left Crete as fast as their sails and oars could take them.

Along the way, they hit horrible weather, and the sky turned completely black, as if it were the middle of the night. Jason respectfully asked the god Apollo to help and guide them, for the area was full of reefs and shoals—treacherous sea rocks above and below the sea surface. Apollo granted Jason's request for help. He came and seated himself on an islet, and this little island became all bright and luminous as if it were made of fire. With this the Argonauts had no problem seeing clearly all around them and avoiding the visible reefs and the invisible shoals. Since then, this little island has been called Anaphe, meaning "lit up" in Greek.

All the Argonauts were visited by visions and dreams while asleep. Some of those dreams had a special meaning and significance, and many of them helped the sailing comrades along the way. That is why they had all gotten into the habit of relating their dreams to one another and of interpreting them as far as they could. Still, one of Euphemos's dreams was very different from all others.

Euphemos was carrying with him a lump of earth that he had taken from the land of Libya. He kept it hidden near his chest inside a little pouch. In his dream, this lump of earth had turned into a beautiful girl.

"I'm the daughter of Triton and Libya," she said. "Please be so kind as to throw me back into the sea again. I want to go and join my people."

When he heard Euphemos's dream, Jason advised him to drop the lump of earth into the water because that was probably the wish of some deity of the sea. Standing on the stern of the *Argo*, Euphemos dropped the pouch containing the lump of earth into the sea. An island arose from the water, and this island was so beautiful that they called it Kalliste, which in Greek means the "fairest." Later on, this island was renamed Thera, or Santorini, as we know it today.

At long last, the *Argo* arrived at Iolkos in the darkness of night. There, very bad news awaited Jason. Hardly had he set foot in the harbor than he was informed that the evil Pelias had killed his entire family. His father, his brother, and his young children had all been slain.

In great pain, sad, and angry at the same time, Jason reached out for the compassion and support of his comrades, the Argonauts. They all sat together contemplating how to punish Pelias. Most of them suggested bringing their own armies from their homelands and launching an attack against Pelias. However, Jason could not afford to wait for the armies to arrive.

"But we men number only fifty, and Pelias will set all his forces against us," remarked the most cool-headed among them. Medea, who all that time was listening without uttering a word, interrupted their discussion, saying:

"Leave that to me. I carry with me such poisonous drugs that Pelias's punishment will be very dire. You all stay here, and the moment you see smoke coming out of the palace, come and meet me there," she instructed them. Hiding somewhere in the ship, she secretly spread a magic ointment all over her body, and in a couple of seconds she had transformed herself. She now appeared to be a very old lady. She then took off her royal attire and dressed herself as a priestess. Inside a hollow little statue of the goddess Artemis, she hid her fearful poisons. Clutching the statuette tightly against her bosom, Medea left the boat at the break of dawn and wandered along the streets of Iolkos. She reached the palace and asked to see the king.

"The goddess Artemis has sent me here to offer you back your youth because you are a good and pious man," she told the king.

"I thank you, but how am I to know that you have the powers to do such a thing?" asked Pelias.

"I will transform myself into a young woman first, so that you can see me with your own eyes, and that will make you believe me," Medea said and then asked to be given some lukewarm water. There, in front of the astonished king, she rinsed the magic ointment from her body and immediately regained her youthful appearance.

Pelias, having seen what happened, told her that he was willing to do whatever she asked him. By then he did not have the slightest doubt that this woman was a witch or an enchantress.

"I want to see and talk privately to your three daughters," replied Medea.

As soon as they were brought to Medea, the three girls were terrified to hear her say to them that if Pelias were to regain his youth, he first had to be killed by the hands of his offspring.

"You must kill him while he is asleep. Then, you must chop him up into very small pieces and boil him in water together with these magic drugs I will give you."

To make them agree to murder their father, Medea had to hypnotize the three girls and make them "see" their sleeping father as a slaughtered lamb. As if in a dream, Medea led the three girls to the highest room of the palace, where they lit torches, supposedly to offer thanks to the goddess who was going to perform the miraculous deed of restoring Pelias to his long-gone youth.

As soon as the Argonauts saw smoke coming out of the palace, they all set off to march there and seize the royal throne. Pelias's daughters slowly came back to their senses, recovering from the mesmerizing fit that had overtaken them. Fully awake now, all three of them realized what they had done. When they saw the Argonauts appearing in front of their eyes, they thought that they were hallucinating and seeing ghosts because everyone believed all of them were dead by now. The three girls turned completely insane and began running all over the palace, hollering, screaming, and blubbering gibberish.

Jason had exacted his revenge. He had avenged the slaying of his family. However, he had no desire to stay at Iolkos any longer. He left the throne to Akastos, the only son of Pelias, and, together with Medea, departed for Corinth, where they settled. The Argonauts, at long last, returned also to their own homelands. The most adventurous and exciting expedition of all the ages was over.

The End

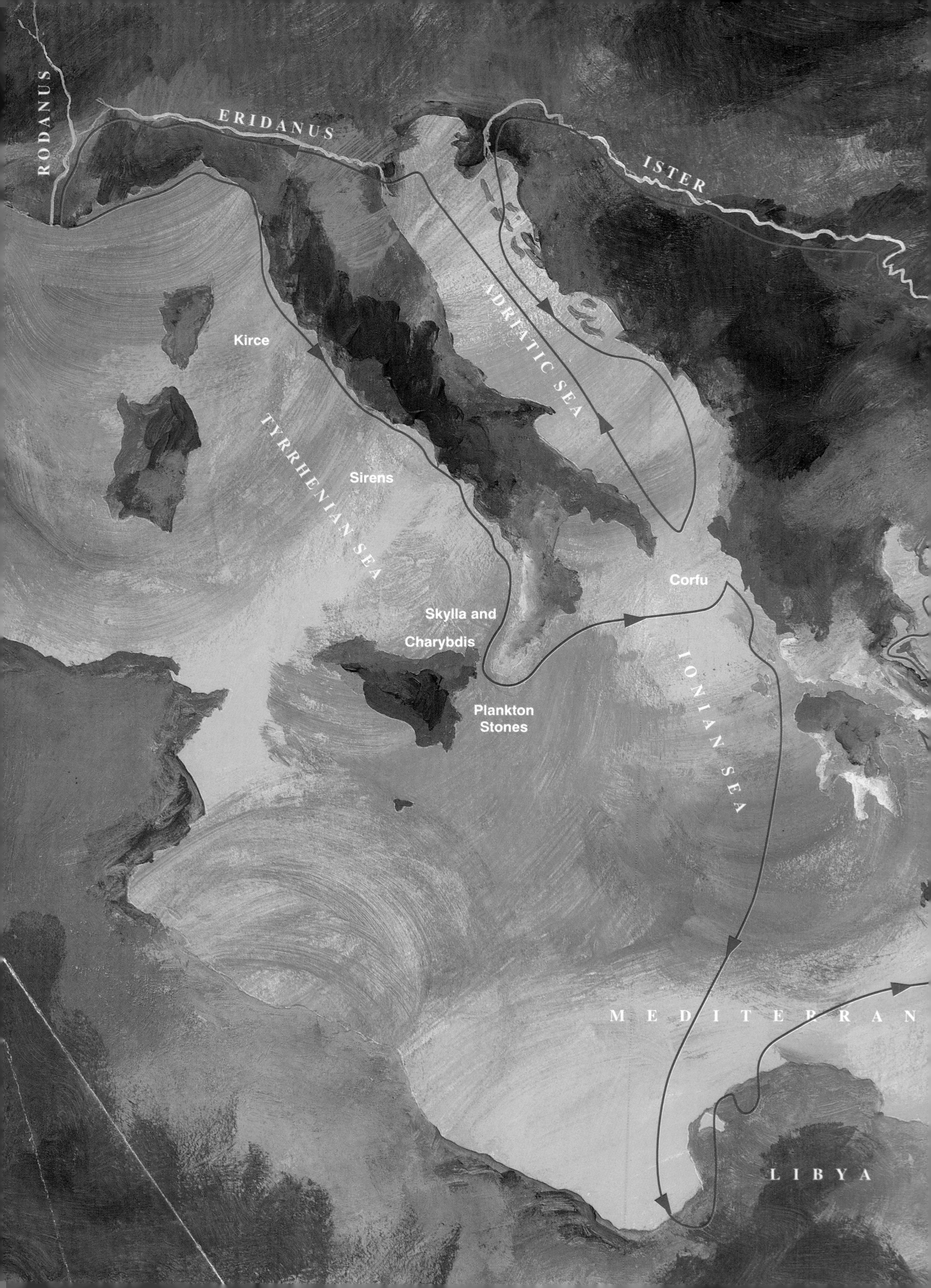

RODANUS

ERIDANUS

ISTER

Kirce

ADRIATIC SEA

TYRRHENIAN SEA

Sirens

Corfu

Skylla and
Charybdis

Plankton
Stones

IONIAN SEA

MEDITERRAN

LIBYA

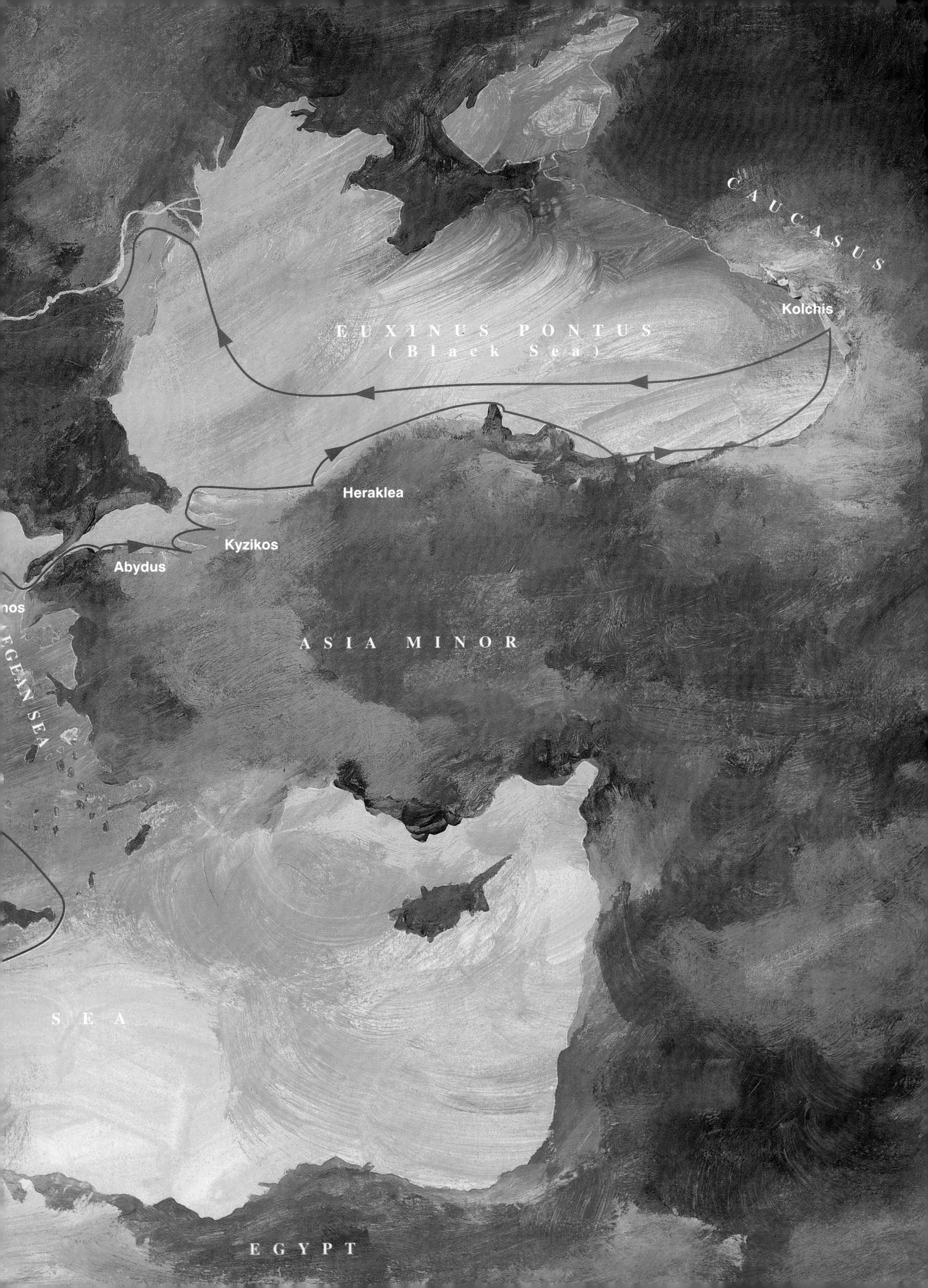

CAUCASUS

Kolchis

EUXINUS PONTUS
(Black Sea)

Heraklea

Kyzikos

Abydus

ASIA MINOR

AEGEAN SEA

nos

SEA

EGYPT

First published in the
United States of America in 2004 by
Getty Publications
1200 Getty Center Drive, Suite 500
Los Angeles, California 90049-1682
www.getty.edu

Publisher: Christopher Hudson
Editor in Chief: Mark Greenberg

Translator: Mary Perantakou-Cook
Managing Editor: Ann Lucke
Editor: Mollie Holtman
Production Coordinator: Anita Keys
Designer: Jim Drobka

Library of Congress Cataloging-in-Publication Data

Zarabouka, Sofia.
    [Argonautiki Ekstrateia. English]
    Jason and the golden fleece : the most adventurous and exciting expedition
of all the ages / Sofia Zarabouka ; translated by Mary Perantakou-Cook.
        p. cm.
Originally published in Greek in 1993.
ISBN 0-89236-756-3 (hardcover)
1. Jason (Greek mythology)—Juvenile literature. 2. Argonauts (Greek
mythology)—Juvenile literature. [1. Jason (Greek mythology) 2. Mythology,
Greek.] I. Perantakou-Cook, Mary. II. Title.
BL820.A8Z37 2004
398.2´0938´02 — dc22

                                    2003025938

Printed and bound in Greece by Kedros Publishers

£24.99

Tanger
Tetouan
Asilah
Chefchaouen
Oujda

Rabat
Kenitra
Fès
Meknes

Khenifra

Er Rachidia
Boudnib
rakech

arzazate

Zagora